A Lottie Lipton ADVENTURE

The Egyptian Enchantment

To Harry & George Edwards

This Americanization of *The Egyptian Enchantment: A Lottie Lipton Adventure* is published by Darby Creek by arrangement with Bloomsbury Publishing Plc.

Darby Creek
A division of Lerner Publishing Group, Inc.
241 First Avenue North
Minneapolis, MN 55401 USA

For reading levels and more information, look up this title at www.lernerbooks.com.

Main body text set in Stempel Schneidler Std Roman 12/24.
Typeface provided by Adobe Systems.

Library of Congress Cataloging-in-Publication Data

The Cataloging-in-Publication Data for *The Egyptian Enchantment: A Lottie Lipton Adventure* is on file at the Library of Congress.
ISBN 978-1-5124-8182-2 (lib. bdg.)
ISBN 978-1-5124-8188-4 (pbk.)
ISBN 978-1-5124-8194-5 (EB pdf)

Manufactured in the United States of America
1-43161-32923-3/10/2017

A Lottie Lipton ADVENTURE

The Egyptian Enchantment

Dan Metcalf

ILLUSTRATED BY
Rachelle Panagarry

darbycreek

MINNEAPOLIS

Contents

Chapter One
London, 1928

Lottie bit her lip and frowned in concentration. This was the hardest puzzle she had ever had to solve and she knew that if she got it wrong, she would be in deep trouble. She sighed and read through it again:

If a train leaves Station A traveling at 70 miles an hour, and another train leaves Station B traveling at . . .

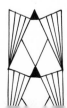

"Argh!" she moaned. "Why does Uncle Bert always set the *hardest* homework?"

Lottie was sitting at a coffee table in the middle of the small, untidy apartment that she shared with her great uncle Bert. She looked around at the mess: piles and piles of books, shelves crammed with ancient artifacts that Uncle Bert had collected on his digs in Egypt, and photographs of his time in Africa. Her eyes rested on a picture of Uncle Bert with a young, smiling couple in the desert. They were her parents, but they had been killed in an accident when a tomb they were exploring caved in. Her great uncle Bert had taken Lottie back to London, where he had managed to get a job and a place to live in the greatest museum in the world—the British Museum.

Living in the museum had its perks: Lottie could roam the halls when the public had gone home, she could read any book she liked from the vast library, and she didn't even have to go to school! Although sometimes she wished she did, as the lessons that Uncle Bert gave her were getting harder and harder. She tried to read the question again, but all the words jumbled up in front of her eyes, so she stepped away for a while.

It was Sunday morning and the museum wasn't yet open to visitors. The sunlight came streaming in through the apartment window, and Lottie decided that a walk around the museum would be just the thing to clear her head and make her brain work again.

As Lottie walked down one of the many halls that filled the museum, mulling over her tricky homework, she heard a call come from the main entrance hall: "Lottie? Is that you? Come and give me a hand!"

Lottie jogged over to where the sun rolled in through the museum's large open doors. Giant pillars reached up to the high

ceiling. Standing in the main entrance was Uncle Bert. He was a round fellow with a bushy, white moustache and a face that went pink when he got excited, like he was getting right now. He stood over a large wooden packing case with a crowbar in his hand.

"How's the homework going, my dear?" asked Uncle Bert.

"Um . . . fine. Almost done!" Lottie fibbed. "Ooh! Is this a new exhibit?" she asked, quickly changing the subject and succeeding in stopping Uncle Bert from asking any more homework-related questions.

Uncle Bert nodded excitedly. "My friends in Cairo sent it to me. It will be the centerpiece to my new collection," he said proudly.

Uncle Bert set about opening the wooden packing case like a giddy child on Christmas. Within minutes he had managed to lift off the lid, and the sides of the packing case fell away to reveal the treasure inside.

"Wow," gasped Lottie. "An Egyptian mummy!"

A large sarcophagus now lay before them. It was a stone coffin, painted gold and decorated with pictures and symbols. A face was drawn on the top: an image of a sleeping woman.

"This was a rich lady. She died around three thousand years ago," explained Uncle Bert. "She was found in a tomb in Egypt that some of my friends discovered. She was surrounded by her special treasures when they found her."

"Amazing," said Lottie. She approached the sarcophagus to get a closer look but hit her toe on a smaller box. "Ow! What's this?"

"Ah yes, that. Why don't you open it and find out for yourself, my dear?" said Uncle Bert, handing her the crowbar. She began to pry the nails out of the top of the wooden box. With a *POP!* the lid came off, revealing what was inside.

"Ah!" exclaimed Lottie. "Dolls!"

"Pah! Dolls indeed," scoffed Uncle Bert. "These, my dear, are *shabtis*."

Lottie carefully took one of the little models out of the box. It was about the same size as a doll but made of clay. It had

writing all over its body and its arms were folded like a mini mummy.

"When the ancient Egyptians died, they believed that they went to an afterlife where the god Osiris would make them work on the land. Rich people were buried with shabtis, who would come alive and do the work for them. Poppycock, of course."

Lottie was fascinated by the shabtis. She ran her fingers over the engraved writing.

"What is the writing, Uncle Bert?"

"Hmm? Oh, just a spell," said Uncle Bert. He was busy throwing the wood shavings and crumpled up paper that surrounded the sarcophagus over his shoulder.

Wow! A spell! thought Lottie, and she almost dropped the shabti in excitement.

"What on Earth is going on?" came a bellow from behind them, interrupting Lottie's train of thought.

Oh no, thought Lottie. *It's Sir Trev!*

Sir Trevelyan Taylor, the Head Curator of the museum, was the grumpiest man that Lottie knew. He hated Uncle Bert and Lottie living at the museum and was always trying to come up with new ways to get them thrown out. He came striding toward them, wearing a dapper blue suit.

"Professor West! What is this mess?" he barked.

"This mess, as you call it, is a three-thousand-year-old mummy. We're very lucky to have it at the museum," said Uncle Bert, his moustache twitching with annoyance.

"But you're blocking the main entrance! You should have unpacked this in the Egyptology section," Sir Trevelyan cried.

He had a point. Lottie looked around at the dismantled packing crate and wood shavings scattered across the floor. It would take ages to clear it up.

"I'll get a broom," sighed Lottie.

"You'd better be quick," sneered Sir

Trevelyan. "In one hour, the most important people in London will be coming through that door for a donors' meeting. They are very rich and with any luck will give lots of money to the museum. I will *not* be impressed if they have to step over your rubbish. So you had better get it cleared up. *Now!*"

"Or what? You'll give Uncle Bert the sack?" snapped Lottie. She was fed up with Sir Trevelyan threatening them every time he got angry.

"Oh no," grinned Sir Trevelyan. "I'll give *him* the sack!"

He spun around and pointed at a door, where Reg the caretaker had just appeared, holding a broom and innocently munching on a sandwich.

"Did somebody mention a broom?" Reg said around a mouthful of bread.

"That's not fair!" said Lottie. "You can't fire Reg for a mess he didn't make!"

"Why not?" said Sir Trevelyan with an evil laugh. "He *is* the caretaker, after all. He should be keeping the place tidy. And anyway, whenever I threaten Professor West's job and home, you always seem to wriggle out of it. Let's see how you do trying to save someone else's skin for a change."

He marched away, leaving Lottie and Uncle Bert making faces behind his back.

"Don't worry, you two!" said Reg. "I'll get this lot cleared up in a jiffy."

"Reg, dear boy, it's not your fault. We should be clearing it up," said Uncle Bert.

It simply isn't fair. Why does Sir Trev have to be so nasty all the time? thought Lottie. She looked around at the mess that now filled the entrance hall, trying to think of a way out of this situation. Suddenly Lottie had an idea.

"If I can read the spell on the shabti, then maybe I can get them to do our clearing up for us," she muttered to herself. She looked down at the shabti she was still holding in her hands. *Could it work? Probably not. No. Definitely not,* she thought. *But it's worth a try.*

She placed the shabti she was holding gently back in the box so she could pull her trusty detective's notebook from her cardigan pocket. She flipped through it to find the right page. She had all sorts of information in her notebook: telephone numbers, important dates, even ways to say, *Stop! You're under arrest!* in fifty different languages. She also had a key to decipher Egyptian hieroglyphics that she had copied from one of Uncle Bert's many books:

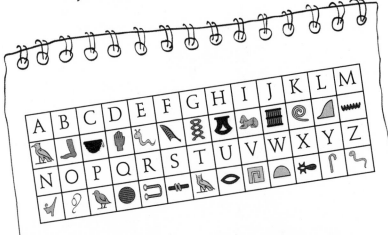

While Uncle Bert muttered about Sir Trevelyan being a nincompoop and Reg started to sweep up, Lottie began to write down and translate the spell:

Can you decipher the spell? Turn the page to see if you're right.

Lottie bit the end of her pencil as she tried to work out the spell.

"Hmm . . . the first letter seems to be *L*, and the next is *E. Lem? Led?* Ah, I see! *Let!*"

Once she had the hang of it, she translated the spell in no time. She was ready to give it a try and cleared her throat.

"Ahem, ahem," she said in a grand way. *"Let the shabtis awake and be free!"*

Electricity filled the air as she said the words, and the box of shabtis started to shake and bounce around on the floor.

"What the 'eck is going on?" shouted Reg.

Lottie began to worry. "Um . . . I was just

trying a spell," she said with a foolish grin.

"You tried a *WHAT*?"

Chapter Two

KA-POW!

An emerald light exploded from the box of shabtis, which shook and bounced on the floor. Lottie backed away, scared of what she had done. Suddenly the shabtis seemed to leap from their box and clatter on the floor. Reg and Uncle Bert watched openmouthed as the shabtis glowed with energy.

"Oh 'eck!" shouted Reg. "They're alive!"

And they were. Each shabti crackled with electricity and began to stand. They stretched their tiny arms and legs and looked around.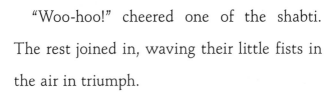

"Woo-hoo!" cheered one of the shabti. The rest joined in, waving their little fists in the air in triumph.

"Woo-hoo! Woo-hoo! Woo-hoo!"

Lottie, Uncle Bert, and Reg stood back from the little crowd of twenty or so shabtis. The little Egyptian servants looked at Lottie and seemed to clap their tiny hands together.

Then, faster than anything Lottie had ever seen before, they all sped out of the main entrance hall and into the museum.

Lottie stood very still, listening to the squeaking voices of the shabtis as they ran farther into the museum.

"Lottie," said Uncle Bert. "What on Earth did you do?"

"Nothing," said Lottie. "I just read the spell on the front of the shabti. *Let the shabtis awake and be free.*"

Uncle Bert frowned and scratched his head.

"You didn't then continue on to the back?

22

If I remember correctly, the whole spell says, *Let the shabtis awake and be free from the spell, ready to serve me.*"

Lottie thought about it. *Oh no!* Instead of making tiny servants that would follow her orders, she had set them free to do whatever they wanted!

"If Sir Trev doesn't like a mess, he really won't like a bunch of magical dolls running loose in his museum," Reg pointed out. "We'd better get after them!"

They raced off in the direction they had last seen the shabtis headed, running through the exhibits and into the library.

"Aaagh!" cried Lottie. "Mess! Everywhere!"

Piles of books lay open on the floor, having fallen from the shelves. The shabtis were climbing up the shelves, throwing books all over the room.

"Hey! You! Get down from there!" shouted Uncle Bert. He then ducked as a book on the history of Rome came flying toward his head.

"Wicked little tykes, ain't they?" said Reg.

Lottie watched as one of the shabtis seemed to shout at the others in a strange, squeaky voice. It was a language she couldn't understand. He was standing on top of a tall set of shelves. He shouted some more and pointed toward the far door. The rest of the

shabtis stopped what they were doing and followed his order, jumping off shelves and running toward the far door.

"He's the leader!" called Lottie. "I'll grab him!"

She darted toward the crowd of living dolls, leaping over desks and sofas. She reached the shelving that he was on and began to climb. The shabtis on the ground shrieked a warning at their leader. But it was too late. Lottie reached out and grabbed the tiny doll.

"Got you!" she said triumphantly. "Now, there has been an awful mistake, I—"

Lottie was interrupted by the leader

yelling at her in his strange language. Even though she couldn't understand him, she could still tell that most of the words he was yelling were insults.

Lottie tried to carry on. "I meant to ask you to help tidy up, but I freed you instead. I think we should—"

She was interrupted again by a long raspberry from the little figure. The crowd of shabtis below laughed and cheered. Lottie was about to tell him off when he opened up his mouth and bit down hard into the skin on her finger.

"Ow!" she screamed. She dropped the shabti, who landed with ease on the ground.

The crowd of shabtis cheered and ran out of the room again, leaving the library a mess. Lottie climbed down.

"Now what?" asked Uncle Bert.

"Well, I've tried talking to them," said Lottie. "But that clearly didn't work. We need a Plan B."

"I've got loads of mousetraps in my cupboard," suggested Reg, rubbing his hands together with excitement. "I could round up the little blighters and trap them."

"Oh no! We can't hurt them," said Lottie, nursing her bitten finger. "We just need to get them back into their box."

"If we can do that, I may be able to find a spell to turn them back to clay," said Uncle Bert. "But we've got to find them first. Which way did they go?"

They followed the shabtis out of the same door they had just run through and down a corridor. Around them, the museum was in tatters. Display cases lay on their sides, the paintings were wonky on the wall, and every last guidebook had been shredded by the shabtis' tiny hands.

"The good news is, I know where they've gone," said Reg. "The bad news is, they've gone down to the basement."

Lottie groaned. The basement held the museum's archives—rows and rows of shelves of old exhibits, files, and boxes. It was a mess to start with, and Uncle Bert had once gotten lost down their for six whole hours!

Lottie gulped. "I suppose we'd better go down there then. Good luck, gentlemen."

Can you find your way through the maze?

Turn the page to find out if Lottie, Uncle Bert, and Reg can make it through the basement!

They agreed to stick together, with Lottie leading the way. They all held hands to stop them from getting separated. Lottie could hear the impish shrieking of the shabtis as they hurried through the miles and miles of shelving.

"I think we're getting closer," said Lottie. "Agh! Dead end."

They turned around and began to run to keep up with the sounds of the chattering shabtis. Every now and then they would come across a shelf that had been pulled over to slow them down.

"It's an awful mess down here. Whose job is it to keep it organized?" asked Uncle Bert.

"Yours!" replied Lottie and Reg at the same time.

They rushed and raced through the basement and eventually found the way out. It was clear that the shabtis had definitely found the way out too, as they could see tiny footprints in the dust on the steps leading up to the ground floor.

"I'll be glad to get out of here," said Lottie. "But I'll be even happier when we catch the little devils!"

Chapter Three

Stepping up into the light of the ground floor, Lottie, Uncle Bert, and Reg walked out of the building and into the sunshine of the large main courtyard. They all paused to catch their breath.

"Is there any way this day could get worse?" said Uncle Bert, panting.

Just then, Sir Trevelyan Taylor walked out of his office.

"Of course it could," grumbled Lottie.

"You three! Get back to work!" came a call from across the courtyard. Sir Trevelyan Taylor waved as he walked toward them. "The main entrance is still a mess and the donors are arriving at twelve o'clock sharp."

Reg was bent double, huffing and puffing.

"All right! Keep your hair on!" he panted. Sir Trevelyan's face dropped into a scowl and he jabbed a finger at Reg.

"Do I need to remind you that your job is on the line?" he growled. "You should remember who runs this place."

Reg frowned and stepped forward, so that he was nose to nose with Sir Trevelyan.

"And *you* should remember who has keys to your office and a pot of quick-drying glue," he muttered. "Watch where you sit, Sir Trev, or you may be stuck there for a long time."

Sir Trevelyan gulped. Lottie put her hand over her mouth, trying not to laugh. Reg was the gentlest man she knew, but he could be pretty terrifying when he wanted to be.

"J-just get it cleaned up," stammered Sir Trevelyan, mustering as much bravado as he could. He turned and walked briskly away. As soon as he was out of sight, Lottie burst out laughing.

"Good one, Reg!" she smiled. "Now, what are we going to do about those silly statues?"

There was a crash from inside the museum. It was the sound of something very old and expensive being knocked over.

"Follow the chaos, I suppose," said Uncle Bert. They quickly ran back into the museum.

Reg kicked open the doors and the three of them followed the racket made by the mischievous shabtis into the Ancient Japanese department. A samurai suit and a priceless old bell from a royal palace lay on their sides. At the far end of the room, a crowd of giggling shabtis were trying to push over a large statue of a dragon.

"Oi!" yelled Reg. The shabtis turned to face him. *"Hands off!"*

The shabtis laughed in their squeaky voices and ran away through a door at the far end of the room.

"Quick!" called Lottie. "After them!"

They dashed across the room. Lottie leaped over the suit of armor and slid on the

polished floor, while Uncle Bert and Reg went around the sides of the room. They came to the open door and Lottie raced through.

Inside was dark and cold.

"Aha! We've got you now!" she called.

She could hear the shabtis. They were close by and making a lot of noise. She felt something brush against the side of her leg— they were around her feet! She was about to reach down and grab one when she was hit from behind by Uncle Bert's large round tummy as he ran through the door. He was quickly followed by Reg, who crashed into them both.

"Oof! What are we doing in here?" asked Reg. Lottie managed to heave herself off the ground in the dark room. She could hear the shabtis in the dark and caught sight of them running out of the door they had just come through.

"Quick, don't let them shut the—" There was a loud *slam*. "—door. Drat!"

The three of them stood in the dark, each searching for the door.

"Where on Earth are we?" said Uncle Bert. There was a fumble and a click. A light came on from above. A tiny light bulb swung above their heads.

"The storage cupboard," said Reg, holding

the end of the cord that switched the light on.

Lottie looked around. It was a small, walk-in cupboard with shelves around each side. There were ancient artifacts, bottles of cleaning supplies, a few old books, and the door behind them, which was now firmly shut. Reg pushed on the handle.

"Do you want the good news or the bad news?" he said.

"Bad," said Lottie, wondering how bad it could be.

"We're locked in, and I don't have keys for this door," Reg said.

"That's pretty bad," said Lottie. "What's the good news?"

"I've got a ham sandwich in my pocket, so we won't starve to death."

Lottie groaned. This was just *perfect*.

"Why don't you have a key?" moaned Uncle Bert. "I thought you could get into anywhere in the museum."

Reg pointed to the door. There was no keyhole. Instead there was small metal panel in place of it.

"When they built this room originally it was to store an ancient and extremely valuable jewelry exhibit. So they wanted it to be extra secure. They fitted it with a combination lock on the outside to keep out any unwanted intruders. But maybe if I unscrewed this panel . . ."

Reg pulled out a screwdriver from his pocket and began to take the screws off the small metal panel on the door. In a few minutes he had removed it, and Lottie squeezed past Uncle Bert to take a look.

Behind the panel was a grid with a series of numbers printed inside small squares. In three of the squares were brass dials, which Lottie found could be moved to display any number.

"If I remember correctly, you have to put the right number in the blank spaces, so that each line going up and down, and left and right, adds up to ten," said Reg over her shoulder.

"Off you go, then," said Lottie, standing up and moving out of the way for Reg. Reg blushed.

"Math was never my strong subject at school, Miss Lottie."

Lottie looked at Uncle Bert.

"Um, maybe you should try this one, my dear," he said, embarrassed that he couldn't work it out. Lottie sighed and looked closely at the grid.

"It's up to me, then," she said. "Eek!"

3	1	
	6	2
5		2

Can you help Lottie?
Make sure each row and
column add up to ten.

Good luck! Turn the page
to see if you're right.

Lottie sat on the floor and concentrated. This was going to be hard. She couldn't admit to Uncle Bert that she'd been struggling with her math homework that very morning—then he'd know that she had lied to him! She'd just have to take it step by step. She took a deep breath.

3+2+1=
6+3+2=

Using her fingers and thumbs to count, and a pencil from Reg's pocket to doodle problems on the door, she started to get results.

"Hmm . . . so if I put a three there . . . and a two here . . ." she mumbled to herself.

"Um, Lottie dear. I don't wish to rush you . . ." said Uncle Bert.

"Then don't!" snapped Lottie.

"It's just that it's getting closer to noon. And we still have to catch the shabtis."

Lottie took a deep breath and rolled the dials around to the numbers she hoped were right.

3	1	**6**
2	6	2
5	**3**	2

There was a whir and a click, and the door sprang open.

"Hooray!" cheered Reg. "Well done, Miss Lottie!"

But Lottie did not cheer. She simply rose up to her full height (which wasn't particularly high) and stepped out of the cupboard. She continued calmly but quickly through the Ancient Japanese department, striding ahead of Reg and Uncle Bert.

"Lottie, my dear, where are you going?" asked Uncle Bert, hurrying to keep up. Lottie replied with a wobble of anger in her voice.

"I'm sick of being given the runaround by a bunch of statues. I'm going to find a solution to this once and for all," she said. She turned to face Uncle Bert and Reg and lifted her head up high, feeling strong and confident. "I'm going to end this."

Chapter Four

Lottie marched back into the main entrance hall, where the mummy still lay in the mess of the open packing case and wood shavings. Uncle Bert and Reg jogged after her, red faced and out of breath.

Lottie looked at the beautiful sarcophagus. Living with Uncle Bert meant she had learned a lot about ancient Egyptians and their mummies. She knew how they preserved the bodies of their loved ones by wrapping them in linen. She knew that they buried the mummies in tombs surrounded by their treasures, which is why grave robbers were always so keen to get inside and steal whatever they could lay their hands on. She knew that a mummy's tomb was supposed to be protected by a curse that meant whoever attempted to get inside would die a horrible death (although she didn't believe that bit).

And she knew that sometimes mummies kept special treasures inside the stone sarcophagus, close to their bodies.

"Open the sarcophagus," she said.

"Lottie! You know as well as I do that we can't just open it up. We have to delicately record everything—take  photographs, measurements, and samples," said Uncle Bert. "Besides, it could be dangerous. It hasn't been opened in three thousand years."

Lottie nodded. She knew all this, but she had another plan up her sleeve.

"Time is running out, Uncle Bert," she pleaded. "If you were buried three thousand years ago with a handful of shabtis to help you when you reached the afterlife, wouldn't you want to keep the instruction manual close by?"

Uncle Bert thought about it and after a few moments seemed to understand.

"You mean . . . a book of spells? In there?" he said, pointing to the mummy. He grinned like a schoolboy who had just scored the winning goal. "Reg! Help me get this open!"

"Right you are, Professor West!"

Reg didn't have a clue what was going on but helped Uncle Bert anyway.

With Uncle Bert at the toes and Reg at the heavier head end, they used crowbars to pry the top of the sarcophagus open and get ahold of the lid.

"One, two, three, *heave*!"

Slowly they managed to slide the lid of the sarcophagus away from the bottom, a horrid scraping noise echoing in the large entrance hall as they did so. Lottie peered over the top. Inside, the mummy was lying still, neatly wrapped in linen, untouched for thousands of years. A scroll was tucked into the side of the coffin, wedged between the mummy and the stone. Carefully, Lottie reached out and took the scroll, teasing it from its resting place.

"Sorry," she whispered to the mummy. "We need to keep your shabtis under control."

She was about to unfurl the scroll to read it, when Uncle Bert placed a hand on her shoulder.

"I'll take that, thank you very much," he said. "Sorry, my dear, but letting you loose with a spell was how we got into this mess in the first place."

Lottie was about to argue, but she realized that Uncle Bert was right. She sat and sulked on a nearby step for a few minutes while Uncle Bert read the scroll. He was such an expert that he didn't even need a notebook to translate the hieroglyphics.

"Hmm . . . yes, I see . . . goodness gracious . . . well, I never," he mumbled to himself as he read it. Lottie and Reg hung on his every word.

"Have you cracked it?" asked Reg. "What does it say?"

Uncle Bert turned to them with a shrug.

"I haven't the faintest idea," he said. Lottie groaned and reached for her trusty notebook to see if she could help.

"I mean, I can translate it, but I don't know what it means."

Reg pulled a pencil out from behind his ear.

"Quick, write it down so we can all have a look."

Uncle Bert borrowed Lottie's notebook and jotted down the spell in his scrappy handwriting. Lottie peered over his shoulder as he wrote. It read:

To stop the shabtis from doing harm,
Find the one who cast the charm.
Add their fingers, ears and nose,
Eyes and arms, mouth and toes.
Take this number and cut it in half;
Halve again, you're on the right path.
Stamp your feet this amount of times,
And call out STOP! to cease their crimes.

Lottie read the riddle through three or four times, just to be sure.

"Miss Lottie, you're the brains of this team," said Reg. "What on Earth does it mean?"

Lottie frowned and shook her head.

"I'm sorry, Reg," she said, deflated. "I don't know."

Can you help Lottie solve the riddle and save Reg's job? Continue reading to see if you're right.

"Come on, Lottie!" urged
Reg. "You can do it. Please,
you're my only hope!"

Lottie looked into Reg's sad
eyes and took a deep breath. *Of course I can
do it,* she thought. *I have to. Just do it step by
step.*

'Find the one who cast the charm.' Well,
that's me! thought Lottie.

*'Add their fingers, ears and nose, eyes and arms,
mouth and toes.'*

Lottie began to worry. She didn't need to
chop them off and brew them in a cauldron,
did she? No, wait! It must mean numbers.
Ten fingers, two eyes, one nose. That makes

thirteen. Add on two eyes, two arms, one mouth, and ten toes.

"That makes twenty-eight," said Lottie aloud.

"Hmm? What does?" interrupted Uncle Bert. "Oh! Ah, I see!"

Lottie waved her hand at him to be quiet while she concentrated.

Half, then halve again.

"Half of twenty-eight is fourteen. Then halve that to make . . ." Lottie faltered.

"Seven!" shouted Reg, looking pleased with himself. "Crikey, that's the quickest bit of math I've done since school!"

Quickly Lottie read through the last part of the riddle. She knew what she had to do. She put her foot forward and stamped on the hard marble floor.

"One . . . two . . . three . . . four," Lottie counted as she slammed her foot down. The sound echoed through the museum. ". . . Five . . . six . . . *seven!*"

Suddenly there was a rush of noise, and Lottie, Uncle Bert, and Reg turned to hear the sound of tiny footsteps charging toward them.

The shabtis came running toward them

and stopped in front of Lottie. They all bowed down to her.

"What's going on?" asked Reg.

"I think . . ." said Lottie with a smile, "I think I'm their leader now."

Chapter Five

The shabtis followed Lottie's every move as she paced the main entrance. Now that they had them under control, there was still all the mess and chaos to clear up. Reg was sweeping up as best as he could, but there was more than he could cope with.

"How long have we got until everyone arrives?" asked Lottie. Uncle Bert looked at his pocket watch.

"Just ten minutes," he sighed. "It can't be done. Reg, it was nice knowing you."

Then an idea struck Lottie.

"Don't give up just yet," she said. She turned to the crowd of shabtis at her feet and put on her most commanding voice. "Oh mighty, mischievous shabtis! If I am your queen, then do my bidding!"

There was a chorus of shabti voices, all seeming to agree.

"Um . . . *Go forth and tidy! Make this museum clean again!*"

Lottie did not know whether it would work, but as she clapped her hands together, the shabtis whizzed off to every

corner of the museum. Lottie stood openmouthed as she heard the sound of every exhibit being put back, every spillage being cleaned up, and the sound of happy shabtis working furiously.

Within minutes the shabtis were back in the entrance hall. They took one look at the mess surrounding the mummy and zoomed over to it. There was a whirlwind of activity—the tiny workers moving faster than the eye could see. In a matter of moments, the entrance hall was clean and sparkling again, and the mummy was back in its packing case.

"Wow," said Lottie, staring at the shining floor and the smiling shabtis. "That was amazing!"

"You can say that again," said Reg. "Can we keep them? It would make my life a lot easier."

"I'm afraid not," said Uncle Bert. "A group of living statues might attract some attention. No, it's best that they rest now."

Lottie and Reg groaned with disappointment. Lottie knelt down to the shabtis.

"Thank you for helping us," she said. The shabtis bowed down to her, and Lottie realized that she might actually miss the cheeky little things. She put her hand out and the leader of the group stepped forward. He climbed onto her palm. "You did a great job, but now it is time to sleep. Sweet dreams."

She passed her hand over the shabti's face and closed his eyes. When she took her hand away, he had turned back to a statue and so had the rest of the group on the floor. She smiled.

"Thank you. All of you."

"Right, you lot!" came the voice of Sir Trevelyan Taylor as he paced through the museum toward the main entrance. "If this place isn't spotless for the donors' meeting, then you're going to pay—"

He turned the corner into the entrance hall, just in time to see Lottie loading the last of the shabtis back into their box and Reg wheeling the mummy's case out of the entrance hall on a trolley.

"Oh," said Sir Trevelyan, a bit disappointed. "How did you do all that in one hour?"

Lottie looked down at the box of silent statues.

"It's amazing what you can do with a little help from your friends," she said.

"I assume Reg's job is safe?" asked Uncle Bert. Sir Trevelyan nodded.

"And you're going to say sorry to him?" said Lottie. She smiled as Sir Trevelyan's face turned red with anger.

"Don't push it!" he growled. "Now get out of my sight!"

"Gladly," said Lottie. She linked arms with Uncle Bert. "Time for a cup of Earl Grey tea, Uncle?"

"Absolutely, my dear."

Reg joined Lottie and Uncle Bert in their small, untidy apartment after he had put the mummy safely away into storage. They all sat on the leather sofa surrounded by Uncle Bert's usual piles of newspapers and books.

"You should have gotten the shabtis to tidy this place up a bit," said Reg.

"It *did* cross my mind," said Lottie.

"Nonsense. Everything is right where I want it," laughed Uncle Bert. "Oh, Lottie, my dear, do you have that homework I gave you?"

Lottie picked up her exercise book from the coffee table and handed it over.

"I think I managed to get it all right," she said with a grin. Uncle Bert looked though the pages.

"Hmm," he murmured. "You did this all by yourself?"

"Of course."

"No help from anyone?"

"No!" said Lottie. "Really Uncle Bert, why would you think such a thing?" said Lottie in a hurt voice.

Uncle Bert put the book down on Lottie's lap. The pages were full of strange scribbles.

"Because it's all in Egyptian hieroglyphics,"

laughed Uncle Bert. "Shabtis may be good at cleaning, but homework isn't their strong point!"

Reg and Uncle Bert laughed while Lottie sighed.

"Drat!" she said. "Silly old shabtis!"

Glossary

chaos: mess and disorder

curator: the manager of a museum

Egyptology: the study of ancient Egypt

hieroglyphics: ancient Egyptian writing that looks like small pictures

mummy: the body of someone who has died that is wrapped in cloth and kept in a good condition

sarcophagus: a large stone coffin, usually decorated

shabtis: small statues that looked like mummies. They were buried with mummies so that they could come to life and be their servants in the afterlife.

Did You Know?

- When the famous Egyptian pharaoh King Tutankhamun died, he had 413 shabtis in his tomb.

- Most shabtis were between four and eight inches (ten and twenty centimeters) tall, but some were as large as twenty-four inches (sixty centimeters).

- Shabtis were made of all sorts of materials: clay, wood, glass, bronze, carved stone, wax, and even mud. The most popular were made from a brightly colored pottery called faïence.

Brain Teaser

Reg has gotten himself locked in the cupboard again! Can you help him complete the puzzle to get out? Put the numbers 1, 2, 3, and 4 into the boxes without repeating any of the numbers in each line going down or across, or in each smaller box.

			2
1			
			3
3			

Crack the Code

Use the key on page 16 to work out the message below. Good luck!

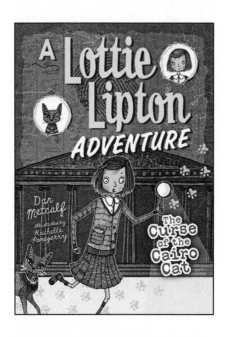

A LOTTIE LIPTON ADVENTURE
The Curse of the Cairo Cat

The Golden Cat of Cairo is missing. Can Lottie Lipton,
nine-year-old investigator extraordinaire,
find it before it's too late?

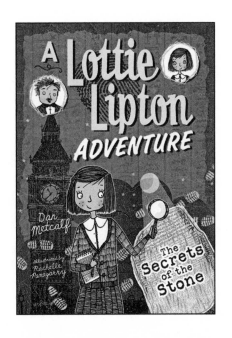

A LOTTIE LIPTON ADVENTURE
The Secrets of the Stone

A mysterious clue appears on the Rosetta Stone.
Can Lottie Lipton, nine-year-old investigator extraordinaire,
solve the clue and beat Bloomsbury Bill?

A LOTTIE LIPTON ADVENTURE
The Scroll of Alexandria

The precious scroll of Alexandria has been hidden for
thousands of years. Can Lottie Lipton, nine-year-old
investigator extraordinaire, track down the missing scroll?

Notes:

Notes:

Notes:

Notes: